· Gordon ·

· Harold ·

· Percy ·

THOMAS THE TANK ENGINE & FRIENDS

Based on
The Railway Series
by The Rev W Awdry

Ladybird Books

Acknowledgment
*Photographic stills by David Mitton and Terry Permane
for Britt Allcroft Ltd.*

British Library Cataloguing in Publication Data

Awdry, W.
    Percy and Harold; Percy takes the plunge.—
    (Thomas the tank engine and friends; 10)
    I. Awdry, W.   II. Series
    823'.914[J]   PZ7
    ISBN 0-7214-1029-4

First edition

© KAYE & WARD LTD MCMLXXXVI
© BRITT ALLCROFT LTD MCMLXXXVI
© In presentation LADYBIRD BOOKS LTD MCMLXXXVII

All rights reserved. No part of this publication may be reproduced, stored in a retrieval system, or transmitted in any form or by any means, electronic, mechanical, photo-copying, recording or otherwise, without the prior consent of the copyright owners.

Printed in England

Percy and Harold

Percy and Harold

Percy worked hard at the new harbour. The men needed stone for their building work.

Toby helped, but sometimes the loads of stone were too heavy and Percy had to fetch them for himself.

Sometimes, as he pulled the trucks along the harbour quay, Percy would see Thomas. "Well done, Percy," Thomas would say. "The Fat Controller is very pleased with us."

5

There was an airfield close to the
harbour. Percy heard the aeroplanes
zooming overhead all day. The noisiest
of all was a helicopter which hovered
overhead, buzzing like an angry bee.

"Stupid thing!"
Percy would say,
as he ran past the
airfield. "Why can't
it go and buzz
somewhere else?"

One day Percy stopped at the airfield. The helicopter was standing quite close.

"Hello!" said Percy. "Who are you?"

"I'm Harold," said the helicopter. "Who are you?"

"I'm Percy. What whirly great arms you've got."

"They're nice arms," said Harold. "I can hover like a bird. Don't you wish you could hover?"

"Certainly not!" said Percy. "I like my rails, thank you."

"I think railways are slow," said Harold. "They're not much use and quite out of date."

Harold whirled his arms and buzzed away.

9

Percy puffed off to find Toby at the quarry.

"I say, Toby," he burst out, "that Harold, that stuck-up whirlibird thing, says I'm slow and out of date. Just let him wait, I'll show him."

Percy collected his trucks and started off, still fuming.

Soon, above the clatter of the trucks, he heard a familiar buzzing.

"Percy," whispered his driver, "there's Harold. He's not far ahead. Let's race him."

"Yes, let's," said Percy excitedly and, quickly gathering speed, he steamed off down the line.

Percy pounded along, and the trucks screamed and swayed as they gathered speed together on their journey through the valley.

"Well, I'll be a ding-dong-danged!" said the driver. There was Harold, high above them — the race was on!

"Go it, Percy!" yelled his driver. "You're gaining."

Percy had never been allowed to run fast before; he was having the time of his life!

"Hurry! Hurry! Hurry!" he panted to the trucks.

"We don't want to, we don't want to," they grumbled.

But it was no use; Percy was bucketing along with flying wheels, and Harold was high above, alongside.

The fireman shovelled for dear life while Percy's driver leant out of the cab window and cheered Percy along. He was so excited he could hardly keep still.

"Well done, Percy," he shouted. "We're gaining! We're going ahead! Oh good boy, good boy!"

Far ahead a distant-signal warned them that the harbour wharf was near. "Peep, peep, peep," whistled Percy. "Brakes, guard, please."

The driver carefully checked the train's headlong speed. They rolled under the main line, and halted on the wharf.

"Oh dear!" groaned Percy, "I'm sure we've lost."

The fireman scrambled to the cab roof. "We've won! We've won!" he shouted. "Harold's still hovering. He's looking for a place to land!"

"Listen boys!" he called. "Here's a song for Percy:

Said Harold Helicopter to our Percy,
    'You are slow!
Your railway is out of date
    and not much use you know.'
But Percy, with his stone trucks,
    did the trip in record time.
And we beat the helicopter
    on our old branch line!"

The driver and the guard soon caught the tune and so did the workmen on the quay.

Percy loved it. "Oh, thank you!" he said. He liked the last line best of all.

Later Percy and Toby went back to the shed. Percy was a very happy engine indeed.

Percy takes the plunge

Percy takes the plunge

One day Henry puffed wearily into the station. He wanted to rest in the shed but Percy was talking to Bill and Ben, the twin tank engines. He was telling them

about the time he had braved bad weather to help Thomas.

"...It was raining hard. Water swirled under my boiler," said Percy dramatically. "I couldn't see where I was going, but I struggled on..."

"Oooh, Percy, you *are* brave," said Bill.

"Well, it wasn't anything really," smiled Percy. "Water's nothing to an engine with determination."

"Tell us more, Percy," said Ben.

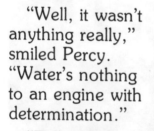

"What are *you* engines doing here?" hissed Henry, suddenly. "This shed is for the Fat Controller's engines. Go away!"

"Silly things," Henry snorted as Bill and Ben ran off.

"They're not silly," said Percy. He had been enjoying himself and was cross because Henry had sent them away.

"They are silly, and so are you,"
muttered Henry. "'Water's nothing to an
engine with determination.' Huh!"

"Anyway," said cheeky Percy. "I'm not
afraid of water. I like it."

Percy ran off to the harbour, singing,
  *"Once an engine attached to a train
    was afraid of a few drops of rain."*

"No one ever lets me forget the time
I wouldn't come out of the tunnel in case
the rain spoilt my paint," huffed Henry.

When Percy reached the harbour he found Thomas on the quay. Thomas was looking at an old board.

It read: DANGER! ENGINES MUST NOT PASS THIS BOARD

"We mustn't go past it," Thomas said. "That's orders."

"Why?" asked Percy.

"'DANGER' means falling down something," replied Thomas wisely.

"I went past 'DANGER' once," he said, "and fell down a mine."

Percy looked beyond the board. "I can't see a mine," he said. He didn't know that the foundations of the quay had sunk and that the rails now sloped downward to the sea.

"Stupid board!" said Percy, crossly.

For days and days afterwards he tried to sidle past it, but his driver stopped him every time.

Then Percy made a plan.

One day, as he made his way to the harbour, he whispered to the trucks, "Will you give me a bump when we get to the quay?"

The trucks were surprised. They had never been asked to bump an engine before. They giggled and chattered about it all the way through the journey.

"The driver doesn't know my plan," chuckled Percy.

"On! On! On!" laughed the trucks. Percy thought that they were helping.

"I'll pretend to stop at the station, but the trucks will push me past the board," he said. "Then I'll make them stop. I can do that whenever I like."

If Percy hadn't been so conceited, he would never have been so silly. Every wise engine knows that you cannot trust trucks.

They reached the quay and Percy's brakes groaned. *That* was the signal for the trucks.

"Go on! Go on!" they yelled and bumped Percy's driver and fireman off the footplate.

"Ow!" said Percy, sliding past the board. The rails were slippery. His wheels wouldn't grip.

Percy was frantic. "That's enough!" he hissed. But it was too late. Once on the

slope, he slithered down into the sea.

Percy was sunk.

"You are a very disobedient engine."
Percy knew that voice. He groaned.

"Please sir," said Percy. "Get me out, sir. I'm truly sorry, sir."

"No, Percy," said the Fat Controller. "We cannot do that till high tide. I hope this will teach you to obey orders."

"Yes, sir," Percy shivered. He was cold. Fish were playing hide and seek through his wheels. The tide rose higher and higher.

It was dark when the men brought floating cranes to rescue Percy.

Percy was too cold and stiff to move by himself, so the next day he was sent to the works on Henry's goods train.

"Well, well, well!" chuckled Henry. "Did you like the water?"

"No!" muttered Percy.

"I *am* surprised," smiled Henry. "You need more determination, Percy. 'Water's nothing to an engine with determination,' you know. Perhaps you would like it better next time."

But Percy is quite determined that there won't be a "next time"!

• Duck •

• Diesel •

• Daisy •